Bear's Den

Written and illustrated by

John Prater

Hamish Hamilton
London

HAMISH HAMILTON LTD

Published by the Penguin Group
27 Wrights Lane, London w8 5tz, England
Viking Penguin Inc., 375 Hudson Street, New York, New York 10014, USA
Penguin Books Australia Ltd, Ringwood, Victoria, Australia
Penguin Books Canada Ltd, 10 Alcorn Avenue, Toronto, Ontario, Canada m4v 3b2
Penguin Books (NZ) Ltd, 182–190 Wairau Road, Auckland 10, New Zealand

Penguin Books Ltd, Registered Offices: Harmondsworth, Middlesex, England

First published in Great Britain by
Hamish Hamilton Ltd 1992

A CIP catalogue record for this book is available from the British Library

ISBN 0-241-13076-X

Set in 15pt Plantin by
Rowland Phototypesetting Ltd, Bury St Edmunds, Suffolk
Printed in Hong Kong by
Imago Publishing

One morning Bear woke to find the sun
streaming into his room.

"Yippee!" he said.

The past few days had been windy and
wet, and he hadn't been able to play
outside.

"I'm going straight to my den," he
thought, as he quickly munched his
breakfast.

The den was Bear's special place, dug
out from the foot of the old oak tree, at the
bottom of the garden.

Everyone knew the den was there, but
Bear was the one who had found it first,
and nobody went in without him.

Sometimes he played there on his own, with his toys.

Sometimes his friends Mole, Dog, and Fox came too; they had picnics together, and invented new games.

Sometimes, (though not very often), he even allowed his little twin sisters in.

Bear finished his breakfast and ran down the garden. He squeezed through the narrow entrance to the den and dropped inside.

But he got a nasty surprise.

Splosh!

The den had been flooded by the rain, and Bear found himself standing in cold muddy water up to his tummy.

"Oh no!" he moaned, looking at the clutter of floating toys, pots and pans, and soggy blankets.

Sadly he paddled around, collecting his things, then plodded back to the house.

Dad was in his workshop, looking at a plan. He seemed rather puzzled, and was muttering quietly to himself. "Now that's that bit . . . I think."

All over the floor were lots of pieces of wood.

When he saw Bear standing miserably by the door Dad whirled round, clutching the plan behind him.

"What's the matter, Bear?" he asked, gently pushing him outside.

Bear poured out his story.

"Right," said Dad. "This wood all came in a great big box. You can have that to play in."

"Great! Thanks, Dad," said Bear, cheering up.

Dad cut a door and window in the box, and pushed it into the garden.

Mum gave him another old blanket, and Bear began to furnish the new den with a few things from the house.

"This is fun," he thought, but then his sisters appeared. When the twins saw the box they wanted to get inside.

"Get off the roof!" yelled Bear, as they clambered over the top.

"Let us in!" they demanded.

"GO AWAY!" shouted Bear.

The twins did leave, but it was only to find some big sticks. Very soon they were back.

"Can we come in?" they asked nicely.

"NO!" said Bear.

The twins started banging the box, and poking their sticks through the window.

Bear was really cross, but had lost too many scraps with his sisters before. He decided to let them in, but made them sit at the other end, and told them to be quiet, or else!

There was a tap, tap, on the door.

"Hello, Bear," said Mole. "I saw what a mess the old den was in, but this looks super. Can I come in?"

Without waiting for an answer, Mole squeezed into the box.

"It's getting very crowded in here," said Bear to his sisters, hoping they would leave.

"It is a bit small," agreed Mole. "I know, I'll dig you a cellar."

Before Bear could say "No thanks", Mole had dived headfirst at the ground, and begun scooping out great lumps of earth with his big paws. Most of it went over Bear.

"Stop!" spluttered Bear, spitting dirt out
of his mouth. "Look, the box is sinking."

He was right. The den was tilting over,
and disappearing into the hole Mole had
made.

"Sorry, Bear," said Mole, surfacing again.

They all climbed out, and between them pulled the box out of the hole to another part of the garden. They set it up again, and scrambled back inside.

"Who wants a sweet?" asked Mole.

"Sweet?" said a voice outside.

Dog stuck his nose through the door. "I'll have one please," he said as he wriggled into what was now a very full den.

Mole gave everyone a minty chew, and
Dog chomped it noisily.

"Mint, my favourite!" said Fox, who had
also come to play. He shoved his long snout
through the window.

"Don't come in!" shouted Bear, but he
was so squashed his voice came out as a
little squeak. It was too late.

As Fox tried to get inside the box, the sides bulged, and then burst open. The gang tumbled into a heap.

18

"Now you've ruined it," said Bear.

"Never mind," said Mole. "We'll make another one."

"Yes," said Dog, "let's find some things and make a really BIG den."

Bear returned to the workshop.

"Now what?" asked Dad, standing in front of his workbench.

Bear explained what had happened.

Dad let him take some pieces of wood from the scrap box, and shooed him away.

Then Dad spotted the twins carrying out a lovely piece of green wood. He snatched it back, and told them sternly that he didn't want to be bothered again as he was very busy. He did give them some scraps of hardboard though and they went away happily.

A pile of wood, plastic, rope, boxes, and odds and ends was growing in the garden, as the friends brought things for the new den.

"OK, we've got enough," said Fox.

Cheerfully they began banging and tying, snipping, glueing, tearing and pulling. Everyone worked hard for a whole hour, but they did not seem to be making much progress.

Nobody really knew what they were doing.

Nobody had a plan.

The twins started squabbling and taking each other's hardboard.

Mole banged his thumb with a hammer.
The wall that Fox was building fell onto
Dog's head.

Bear sank down for a rest, but found he was sitting in a puddle of glue. He was stuck to a big plank of wood.

"I'M FED UP!" he yelled, trying to pull the plank away.

"So am I," said Mole.

Everyone else nodded; building a den was too difficult . . . and painful.

Slowly they began to clear up the mess. Bear felt so miserable. He had lost his special place and could not find another one.

He trudged back to the house, loaded with bits of wood.

When he reached the workshop door,
Bear dropped everything in surprise.

Dad was just nailing the last piece to the
roof of a den; a large, wooden, wonderful
tree-house den!

"Happy Birthday!" said Dad, grinning broadly. "It's a bit early, but your present arrived this morning, and I've been making up this kit all day. I thought you'd found me out, but you were so busy you didn't notice. What do you think of it?"

"Dad, it's GREAT! Thank you," said Bear.

"Let's put it in the oak tree now," said Dad.

They loaded the tree-house onto a wheelbarrow, and in a very short time had fixed it firmly in the tree.

Bear's friends came back to find Bear
sitting on the little balcony by the door.

"Come on up," he called. "You're ALL
welcome."

Excitedly, they climbed up into the new den. Bear was so happy he didn't even mind his twin sisters arguing about who could sit on the window seat first. The den was his special place, but today he was happy to share it with everyone.